London folk tales for Children

**Illustrated by
Belinda Evans**

London folk tales for Children

Anne Johnson
and Sef Townsend

The
History
Press

First published 2019
Reprinted 2019

The History Press
97 St George'sPlace,
Cheltenham, Gloucestershire, GL50 3QB
www.thehistorypress.co.uk

British Library Cataloguing in Publication Data.
A catalogue record for this book is available from the British Library.

ISBN 978 0 7509 8689 2

Typesetting and origination by The History Press
Printed and bound in Great Britain by TJ International Ltd

Lo

Mayfair
⑧

Kensington
⑦ Gardens

The

Westminster

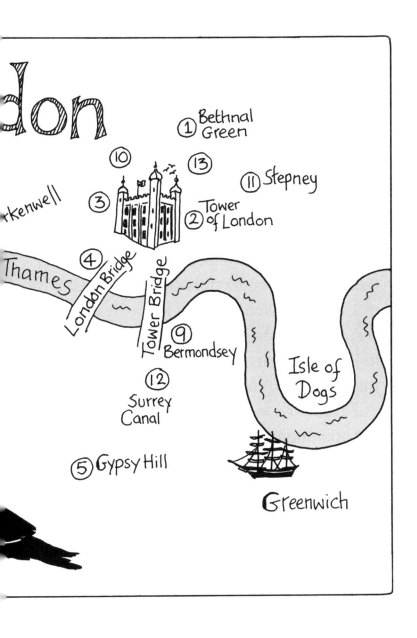

OUR THANKS

Many people have helped us to bring together these tales of London folk and of the great city of London which they call home. It has been very good to share our ideas with them and to listen to their stories and we would like to thank them all for their help.

Farah Naz was reminded of a story that her grandmother told her, while sitting under a magnolia tree in an East End park; John Heyderman shared the story of how his father first came to London after escaping from Berlin at a dark and dangerous time in the past; Pernilla Iggstrom told us of the long journey that brought her to London and of the Korean story that makes her think of her own life; David

Solomon lives in the place in East London where the gasometers and all the surrounding houses were saved from the fire bombs during the Second World War. We would also like to thank Payam Torabi, for his wonderful help and inspiration; Sally and Thom, Toby, Helen, Grace and Iris, who have listened to so many stories and songs and have shared their own with laughter and fun; Becky, Matthew, Iris and May, who were always encouraging; Bol, who has listened with patience and good advice to all the ideas of how to put the book together; and John Chapman, whose journey to London brought him fame and fortune that people talk about 500 years later.

We are indebted to Henry Mayhew, who in the mid-1800s contributed eighty-two articles to the *Morning Chronicle* on 'Labour and the Poor', and who was the first to interview and record their lives; also to Miranda Kaufman for her brilliant book *Black Tudors*, which reclaims the long-forgotten lives of people from Africa who worked and earned in Renaissance England.

A special thank you to the teachers and children of Marlborough and Park Walk Primary schools in the London Borough of Kensington and Chelsea, with whom we have been exploring stories for our shared project 'We Are Londoners', generously funded by John Lyon's Charity. Thank you to the story-tellers and musicians of Everyday Magic who are part of this project and to Holly Johnson for giving us her take on stories in progress.

Anne Johnson and Sef Townsend

ABOUT THE AUTHORS

ANNE JOHNSON has been a Londoner for fifty years. She is a professional storyteller and songwriter who is committed to bringing live storytelling and music into schools as the Director of Everyday Magic, which every year fires the imaginations of over 1,500 children at London schools.

SEF TOWNSEND has been a Londoner for nearly forty years and has been telling traditional tales from around the world almost as long as that. He loves travelling and collecting stories from many countries, but is always surprised to find some of the best stories right here in lovely old London.

INTRODUCTION: STORIES OF LONDON FOLK

London is a city of 9 million people and so it is a place which is full of stories. Stories of all the different people who live here. But if London itself has a story to tell, how does it tell it?

Well, it is told through things that are found on the bed of the river, the River Thames. It is told whenever a new office block or an important building is put up in the city of London. Before the foundations of the building are put down, the ground has to be dug, or excavated, very deep so the building will stand safe and strong. Now, when the workmen are digging, they often find things that have been buried in the earth for thousands of years – from the time of the Romans, or even before the Romans came to this land.

In the river, too, as well as things getting lost, like shields and swords, other items were given as offerings to the gods. Tools have been found in the river from the tiny little farming settlements that were here when ancient people worked the land to grow their food, before there even was a London.

However, it was immigrants – people who came from elsewhere – who made London what it is and who have continued to do so, until today. So, a 'London' folk tale may well have begun in a place far, far away from this city on the Thames which, as Londoners, we all call home.

London is the place where we hear many languages spoken in the street and this has been true since the time of the Romans in the first century AD. This is because, apart from Latin, the Romans spoke languages from the countries that they came from. These were places as far apart as Spain and Greece, Germany, Syria and Carthage, on the north coast of Africa. The Romans who came from these places all brought their own languages with them, speaking Spanish and German, Greek, French and Ancient British. This was as well as Latin, the shared language they used to make sense of and to understand the people from other places in the Roman Empire.

Today there are 300 languages spoken every day in the homes of Londoners and on the streets of this fascinating city. So, when you say 'I am a Londoner', you could say that in many different ways, such as:

আমি একজন ল ন লাক; Abu m Londoner;
Soy londinense; Je suis un Londonien;
أنا لندوني; Jestem londyńczykiem;
Ben bir Londra kişiyim; 我是伦敦人;
Mo wa Londoner kan; Я лондонець;
Tá mé ó Londain; 나는 런던 출신이다.

Do you know any other way of saying 'I am a Londoner'?

This small collection of stories has been put together by Anne and Sef and illustrated by Belinda. We are Londoners with – between us – family roots in Ireland, Wales, England, France, north-eastern Europe and Central Asia. These stories all have a connection to people who lived in London, stretching back to the Middle Ages.

Some of the stories come from Londoners we have spoken to. Some of them are very old tales. One story comes from an old ballad – that is, a story in the form of a song. These ballads were sung and the words to the ballads were sold on the streets of London. Some of these stories are imagined: what would it be like to be a poor child trying to sell watercress on the streets of Victorian London or a boy who worked for a chimney sweep? Some of the stories imagine what London and Londoners might look like to a bird or a creature who've made their home in this city. Some are stories within stories that people have brought with them from other lands.

Anne and Sef both work as storytellers in London schools and we hope this book will encourage you to become a detective and discover some of the stories behind the statues, the street names and the buildings of London. To find out about London, past and present, and the stories of people who have lived here and who live here now.

What better way to share than through stories? We dream stories, we tell stories, we love to listen to stories and people have been telling and listening to stories for thousands of years. We bet you have your own story. The human family is one family and this great family shows its many faces on the streets of London.

London's windblown stories are as countless as the stars.

BESSY OF
BETHNAL GREEN

'Where are you going to my pretty maid?'
'I'm going a milking, sir,' she said,
'Sir,' she said, 'sir,' she said.
'I'm going a milking, sir,' she said.
'Then can I come with you, my pretty maid?'
'You're kindly welcome, sir,' she said,
'Sir,' she said, 'sir,' she said.
'You're kindly welcome, sir,' she said.
'What is your fortune, my pretty maid?'
'My face is my fortune, sir,' she said,
'Sir,' she said, 'sir,' she said.
'My face is my fortune, sir,' she said.
'Then I cannot marry you, my pretty maid.'
'Nobody asked you, sir,' she said,
'Sir,' she said, 'sir,' she said.
'Nobody asked you, sir,' she said.

It was the year 1300 and in Bethnal Green there lived a blind beggar and his wife. He wandered around with a little bell and a dog to guide him. They had a very beautiful daughter named Bessy. She was clever and kind and wanted to be useful to her dear mother and father. She pleaded with them to let her go and seek her fortune. They were unwilling to let her go, but at last after much persuasion Bessy left on foot, carrying what little she owned tied up in a cloth.

She travelled by night so that she would not be seen and rested hidden in the woods by day. It was late summer and the bushes and trees were heavy with berries and fruit, so she had food to eat. There were clear streams of water to drink from and to wash in.

One evening she was sitting by a stream with her feet in the cool, clear water. Her feet were sore after so much walking. She was about to get up and find a place in the woods to sleep, when a young man came out of the woods carrying a large dish of blackberries that he had collected.

He said, 'May I help you? You look as if you have travelled far. My father is an innkeeper,' he continued, 'and our inn, the King's Arms, is only over that hill. My father needs help in the inn. Are you looking for work?'

'That I am,' answered Bessy. 'I will walk with you and meet your father.'

The young man spoke the truth. There was a village the other side of the hill, the village of Romford. Bessy spoke with the innkeeper and found him to be a fair man. He said he would give her a room of her own and her meals and pay her for her work in the inn.

The work was to serve the food and drinks, to wash the mugs and dishes and to keep the place swept and dusted. Bessy agreed and was very happy to have found a place to live and work and where she could save money for her mother and father. The very

first week she was there the young men of Romford came to the inn, not just to eat and to drink but to see Bessy and listen to her singing as she went about her work. The innkeeper was very pleased as the King's Arms was busier than it had ever been and he was making a lot more money.

The innkeeper's son also thought what a good wife Bessy would make. When he became owner of the inn, with Bessy as his wife he would get rich.

Bessy got on well with the innkeeper and his wife. The young men came to the inn with gifts for her but Bessy did not accept them. She was the same to all of them: polite and friendly, but she was not looking for a husband. Still they came, hoping that one day she might change her mind.

One morning a young knight arrived at the inn looking for a stable for his horse, which had become lame. Bessy watched as the young knight led it into the stables at the side of the inn. She saw how he cared for his horse that had a lame leg. She saw how gently he spoke to the small boy who worked in the stable and heard him ask the boy to look after his horse well; and he gave the boy a silver coin. The young knight then came to the inn door and when he saw Bessy, he bowed to her and asked her permission to come in.

'I am very dusty after my long journey and I would not like to spoil this clean floor,' he said.

'Sir,' she said, 'you are very respectful but I only work here and it is my job to clean up after others.'

The knight said, 'I would not wish to spoil your work and I respect a working woman as much as the highest princess in the land.'

'Indeed,' she said, 'you are a true knight,' and Bessy encouraged him to come in and sit down.

The young knight stayed at the inn for many weeks, while his horse's leg healed. Bessy saw how he was gentle and courteous to all. One day a man brought his horse and cart into the stable yard. The man was shouting at the horse and hitting it with a heavy stick. The young knight did not say a word but went into the stable yard and took the stick out of the man's hands and broke it in two. The man swore and shouted.

The knight at first said nothing but then he spoke. 'Your horse is one of God's creatures. Has that horse worked for you for many years?' The man said yes, but now the horse had got lazy and would not pull the cart. The knight looked at the horse and said, 'Your horse has sores on its back where the cart has rubbed it and it is lame in one leg.' The man said he had no money to pay to look after the horse. 'Then I will pay,' said the knight,

'but you must give me your word that you will not ill-treat that horse again.' The man looked ashamed and mumbled his thanks.

The young knight was falling in love with Bessy but he would not say anything until he thought that perhaps Bessy might be getting to like him. He had still not spoken to Bessy about how he felt, when one morning a fine gentleman came into the inn. He was dressed in the latest fashion, fine wool cloak and a silk hat with a feather. His horse had a saddle trimmed with velvet and tiny silver bells. This fine gentleman came into the inn, saw Bessy and straightaway said in a loud voice so that everyone in the inn could hear, 'You are the most beautiful woman I have ever seen. Will you marry me?'

Bessy replied, 'I am not looking for a husband, so thank you, but no.'

The fine gentleman would not take no for an answer and he hung around trying to find an opportunity to speak to Bessy.

The next day a merchant from London came galloping into the inn yard. He leapt off of his horse and called to the stable boy in a loud voice, 'Come here, boy, and be quick about it. I haven't time to lose. I have silks to sell and money to make.'

The merchant marched into the inn, saw Bessy and said, 'Very good, very good indeed. Not only have I made a lot of money on this trip, I think I have now found myself a wife. This young woman will be good for my business.'

Turning towards Bessy, he said, 'Come now, young woman, marry me and I will dress you in the finest silks and satins, brocades and velvets, and you shall have a fine London house to live in.'

'I have no wish to marry,' replied Bessy and she hurried out of the inn and went for a walk by herself.

The young knight had seen all of this. He was angry that these two men had spoken to Bessy in such a way without thinking for one moment what Bessy might want. He was also sad that Bessy had said that she had no wish to marry. 'I cannot speak to her now,' thought the young knight, 'I have no wish to offend her.' The knight's horse was now ready to take to the road again and the knight began to make plans to move on.

But there was another who had been listening to the fine gentleman and the merchant from London. This was the innkeeper's son. He had plans to marry Bessy himself. Bessy had said very little about where she came from, but he thought, 'She is so well spoken and has such fine manners, she must come from a good family. We would make a fine pair and with the inn and with whatever little money and goods she will receive from her family, we will do very well.' The innkeeper's son decided to tell the fine gentleman and the merchant that they could not stay at the inn and they must leave.

There was a big argument. All three men were shouting at each other and then pushing each other and then throwing kicks and punches. Luckily none of them were fighters. The young knight saw that Bessy was returning from her walk. He did not want her to see this commotion. He stepped forward and said, 'If any one of you has proper respect for this young woman, then you will not make such a show of yourselves in the place where she lives and works.' The three turned and looked at the young knight. At first, they made towards him as if to threaten him, but when they saw that he was indeed a proper knight – that is, a man who knows how to fight – and that he was not frightened of them, they backed off.

At that point Bessy came through the door. The young knight could not stop himself. He went down on one knee and said, 'Dear Bessy, I have thought of you night and day. I would like to marry you, but if you tell me no, then I will go away.'

At that the other three also fell to their knees and said, 'He is but a poor knight, what can he offer you?' and each one cried out, 'Marry me,' 'Marry me,' 'Marry me.'

Bessy looked at all four kneeling around her on the floor. She looked from one to the other, then said, 'My father and mother I mean to obey. You must ask them and please them.'

They all replied, 'Where are your mother and father? Where do they live?'

'My father,' Bessy said, 'is easily seen. He is the blind beggar of Bethnal Green. You will have no trouble finding him, you will know him full well. He is always led by a dog and a bell.'

The fine gentleman went pale, the merchant went red, and the innkeeper's son near went off his head. But the young knight said, 'For better or worse, I weigh not true love by the weight of the purse.'

Bessy smiled and her smile said all. She had watched the young knight over the months he had stayed at the inn. She had seen how careful and kind he was. How he was respectful to all whether they were of high or low birth. She had seen how he was not afraid to speak out to protect poor creatures. Neither was he afraid to fight if need be. Most of all, he did not put money above all else.

He stretched out his hand and Bessy took it. 'I will take you to meet my father and mother. I will tell them that I love you and that you are a true knight.'

They travelled together to Bethnal Green. When they arrived, Bessy said, 'Father, Mother, I have brought this young knight to meet you. He is not rich in money but he is a proper man and one that your Bessy would marry. We can work together to make a good life.'

The young knight bowed to Bessy's parents and said, 'It is true that I am not rich but I will give all that I have to Bessy.' He took from the saddlebag on his horse a small leather bag and tipped the silver coins out on to the floor.

Then the blind beggar took from inside his cloak another bag, much bigger, and tipped from it silver and gold coins. More than enough for a great wedding feast. The blind beggar said, 'I lost my sight in battle. I once was rich and proud. I have lived as a beggar for forty years and saved for this day. Daughter, this is for you and I believe you have chosen well.'

Let love be lord of all.

Mary Fillis [born in Morocco 1577]

*'Old Mother Twitchett has only one eye and
a long tail that she lets fly.'*

'I think the wind must live here,' thought Mary,
as she wrapped her shawl tightly around her.
It was December 1584. Mary was seven years
old and had come from Morocco. Her father
had called her Mariam, but in England they
called her Mary. Only last month she had
been alongside her father in the markets of
Marrakesh looking at the heaps of delicious
dates and almonds that were on sale there.
Now the cold wind was snatching the breath
out of her body as she made her way up the
hill from the River Thames towards Mark
Lane, where she worked in the house of John
and Anne Barker.

She could hear the bells of St Olave's
Church strike four o'clock. Four in the
afternoon and it was already getting dark. Her
father had left her with Mrs Barker and Mary
was helping her to look after little Abigail
Barker, who had just been born. Mary didn't

know why her father had brought her from Morocco or why he didn't take her back with him. He didn't say and if anyone else knew the reason, they didn't tell her.

Her father was on a ship with Mr Barker sailing back to Morocco. The ship was loaded with fine woollen material and it would return with sugar, dates and almonds which

the rich people of England, who loved sweet things, would buy. Mary liked sweet things too, and Mr and Mrs Barker had the money to buy them. Mrs Barker had lovely clothes. She wore a gold chain every day. She had two diamond rings and two pearl necklaces.

Mary had decided she would save the money she was earning working for Mrs Barker and when her father came back, maybe they could have their own house. Maybe they would go back to Morocco. 'I am only seven years old,' thought Mary, 'I can't say what is going to happen. Now I must get back to Mark Street. Cook will be waiting for the herring that she asked me to get from the Dutch herring boats moored on the Thames. But oh, it is so cold. I wonder, will the river freeze? This wind has ice in its breath. It is a bully, this wind, trying to push me back down the hill. I don't think cook would have sent me on this errand if she had known how strong the wind is. Everything and everyone is ruffled and blown about.'

Then Mary thought, 'If there were a wind like this out at sea, Mr Barker's ship might lose its way and Father might never get back to London. The sky is so black and the setting sun looks red and angry. The crows are riding the gusts of wind like witches on broomsticks.'

Finally, Mary was back at the house in Mark Street and Cook was making a fuss of her and she could warm herself by the fire. Tomorrow was another day.

The next morning Mary woke and looked out of her small window at the top of the house. The wind was still strong and the clouds looked like shaggy white beasts moving towards the river. She could hear Mr Barker's voice downstairs, so their ship was safe and they were back. Was her father downstairs?

Mary went down to the kitchen. It was warm and cosy. The fire glowed in the grate. Breakfast was laid ready for her and everyone was very quiet. 'Where is my father?' Mary asked. At first no one answered, then Leying, who was from Guinea and also worked for the Barker family, answered, 'Your father has not returned with Mr Barker.' That is all she would or could say. Mary waited to see if anyone could tell her any more but no one did, not even Mr or Mrs Barker.

Winter turned to spring and life went on as it had before, except that Mary did not hear any news of her father. Mary liked to walk by herself and think. Cook liked her and didn't mind if Mary took her time when she went on errands. 'I like to explore,' Mary told cook, and cook said that was fine, just to be sure not to get lost. 'I like going down to the river,' said Mary, 'I like to watch the ships come in and the ferrymen taking people across to the other bank. I like watching the gulls follow the herring boats. They descend from the sky to catch the bits the fishermen throw them. When the tide is out they pick their way across the mud.'

> *How do they do it*
> *with their clean yellow feet,*
> *matching beak,*
> *feathers sleek?*
> *How do they manage not a hint of grime?*
> *Gulls in the tide at springtime.*

'Once I saw a heron fly over. He was silent and grey. The gulls mobbed him and he flew away. I look for him each time I go down to the river.'

Mary stayed and worked for Mr and Mrs Barker and looked after little Abigail.

It was four years since the ship returned without her father and Mary was now eleven. Little Abigail loved Mary and Mary would carry her around, with Abigail clinging to Mary, riding on her back and burying her face in Mary's thick, dark, curly hair.

Mary thought to herself, 'I can now speak their language as well as they can and I am forgetting my own. There is no one else from Morocco in the house. George was from Guinea. He died and is buried in St Olave's Church in Hart Street. Leying and I go there sometimes to put some flowers on his grave. Now Mr Barker has died and Abigail clings to me more than ever. I don't know whether my father is alive or dead. I never knew my mother. Abigail still has her mother and she has me and her family is rich. She will always be looked after. I don't know if Mrs Barker will look after me always. I must make my own living.'

Mary remembered a story her father had told her. It was about the clever Nasruddin. Nasruddin had been turned away from an important banquet because the servant on the door said that he was not dressed grandly enough. Nasruddin went back dressed in his very best clothes and was allowed in. When the food was served Nasruddin began very slowly and carefully to 'feed' his clothes.

He put some of the delicious slices of meat into the top pocket of his silk jacket. He pushed handfuls of salad into the big side pockets of his silk trousers. He decorated the front of his beautiful shirt with dabs of sauce. The guests sitting near him were staring at him. They began to whisper to each other, 'Do you see what that man is doing? He is behaving very strangely.' They moved their chairs as far away from Nasruddin as possible.

The host arrived and Nasruddin was asked to explain his peculiar behaviour. Nasruddin replied, 'I was turned away from this banquet when I first arrived because I was told I was not dressed grandly enough. I returned wearing my very best clothes and was allowed in. I am sure it was not me that was invited to this feast but my clothes, so I am giving the food to my clothes.'

The story always made Mary giggle, the thought of Nasruddin dabbing sauce onto his fine shirt. Mary understood that the story was saying how important it was to some people to have grand clothes, so she thought, 'I look after the beautiful silk and fine woollen clothes that Mrs Barker wears. I have learnt to clean and mend them with the help of Millicent Porter, the dressmaker, who makes Mrs Barker's clothes. I will ask Millicent to teach me to make fine clothes and then I can sell them to the rich men and women of London. My needles and threads will be my friends.

'Tomorrow is another day and I will not always be the little Moroccan, Mary Fillis, who works in the Barkers' fine house. I will work for myself.'

In 1597 Mary did leave Mrs Barker and went to work with Millicent Porter and learnt to make and mend clothes. She lived in Crew's Rents, East Smithfield, which was then in Middlesex, a village surrounded by fields. Mary was baptised on 3 June 1597 at St Botolph's Church, Aldgate.

GO TO
LONDON:
FIND YOUR
FORTUNE

People have been coming to London for hundreds of years to find their fortune. Or at least to try to find a better life than the hard ones that many who lived in the countryside had in Old England. People even said that the streets of London were paved with gold! But, of course, they would realise very quickly if they came to London that this was just not true.

Well, John Chapman, a pedlar, who lived in the little village of Swaffham in Norfolk, had heard people talking about London all his life. About how, around every corner, there was a fortune awaiting – and he just didn't believe it. He was a hard-working man and he would travel the countryside with a basket strapped to his back, filled with little things to peddle, or to sell. As he travelled from place to place he would call at people's houses and sell them buttons and bows, pins and needles, ribbons and shoelaces and all the things that were difficult to find if you lived far away from a village and its little shops.

But even though John worked so hard, times were difficult and not many people had money to spare. Even a bright ribbon or some matching buttons were something special and they were the sort of thing you'd only get if you had a birthday, a wedding or some other special occasion like that. John noticed that fewer people were buying from him. What could he do? He needed to eat. He needed to sell things to make money to buy food. Each year he had a few apples from the crooked old apple tree in his garden, but there weren't many and they didn't last long before he was hungry again.

Well, one night he had a dream and in the dream there was a voice that was saying, 'Go to London Bridge and there you will find your fortune.' When he woke up in the morning he thought, 'Oh, that was a nice dream, but dreams are just dreams. It would be very nice if they came true – but they don't!' Well, it so happened that he had exactly the same dream the next night. 'How very strange!' he thought. But now he began to wonder if there might be something in it and on the third night when in the dream the voice said once more, 'Go to London Bridge and there you will find your fortune,' he knew that he really must go to London.

That very same day, he closed the door of his little thatched cottage, walked past the crooked little apple tree in his garden, went out through the rickety old gate and down a dusty path on to the road to London, with his little dog wagging its tail at his side. For a poor man, without a horse, the only way to travel was to walk. So, John walked and walked, day after day, so glad to have his dog to cheer him, until he finally arrived in the great city of London.

John had never seen so many people in one place, it was so busy! There were carts racing here and racing there and horses and children charging up and down the streets. Then there were street traders calling out their wares at the tops of their voices, 'Who'll buy my herrings?', 'Chairs to mend!', 'Strawberry ripe!', 'Cherries just off the tree!',

'Buy my fat chickens!', 'Kettles and pots to mend!' Everybody, it seemed, was calling out and it was so busy, so deafening, that he just tried to walk away from all the noise and hubbub, when he found himself by the great River Thames. And there in front of him was the famous London Bridge! It was the biggest bridge he had ever seen and he was surprised to see that all along the bridge were shops and houses. It was just like a street that crossed over the river.

But this was where the dream had told him he would find his fortune, so he walked right along the bridge one way and then came back the other way. It was just like being on a street in the city, with so many people walking and shopping and going about their business. But there was no sign of a fortune yet. He looked

over the edge and watched the water flowing under the bridge. He saw all the ships and barges sailing up and down the river. Then he just stood and waited and his little dog snuggled down at his feet.

The next day he did just the same. On the third day he was beginning to wonder if he had been silly to follow a dream for so many miles on the road to this noisy and confusing place. But, after standing around

for most of the day, a shopkeeper came out of his shop and said, 'I've seen you standing on this bridge now for three days. I can see that you're not begging and you're certainly not trying to sell anything, so what are you doing here?' John answered him honestly that he had dreamed that if he came to London Bridge he would find his fortune.

Well, the shopkeeper laughed so much that his sides shook and he said, 'What? Are you really such a fool as to take a journey all the way to London because of some stupid dream? Now let me tell you, you daft country bumpkin, I too have had a dream every night for the last three nights. I dreamed that I was in some place called Swaffham. What a silly name, Swaffham! I'm sure there is no such place with a name like that. But in that dream, there was a little thatched cottage with a dusty path outside it, a rickety old gate and a crooked little apple tree in the garden. Now in the dream I was told to dig under that tree and there I would find a treasure! Ha, ha, ha, ha, ha. Oh, no, no, no! Do you think I'm such a fool as to go all the way to wherever this place is because of some dream? Oh no, not me. I'm not such a fool. I know that dreams are just dreams and they don't come true.'

As the shopkeeper was saying all this, John realised that he was describing his very own crooked little apple tree behind his own rickety old gate, in his very own garden! Then the shopkeeper continued, 'What I think you should do, me old pal, is to go straight back to where you came from, because you're not going to find a fortune here.' John didn't say anything more than, 'Thank you for your advice. I think you're right, I won't find my fortune here, I will go back home straight away.'

But as he stepped from the bridge on to the bank of the river, he suddenly felt that the answer to his dream was coming true. It wasn't at London Bridge that he would actually find his fortune, but it was here that he had found out where his fortune was! He was sure that his fortune would be under the crooked apple tree in his own garden back in Swaffham. His dog gave a little bark and John whistled a happy tune as he made his way back to the road out of London.

And when he did get back to Swaffham, of course, when he dug for it, there was a big pot of gold right there under his tree. He had found his fortune. At last he didn't have to worry about having enough to eat. He would always have some money in his pocket. But he wasn't a greedy man. He wanted to help others and because the people of the village didn't have enough to repair their crumbling old church, he gave money to repair the rotting old walls and to build a brand new roof. The people were so glad that he had shared his fortune with them that they decorated the church with a statue of him and his little dog.

And if you ever find yourself taking the journey from London to Swaffham, you will see that statue for yourself. And that is proof that John Chapman really did exist and he is remembered there as the Pedlar of Swaffham, who found a fortune by following his dream.

'Any old iron,' calls the rag and bone man,
'Bring out whatever you can,
A rusty mangle or a broken pram
And I'll take it away.'

'What do you lack and will you buy?
Eels alive-o or a hot mutton pie,
Lily-white celery or hot sheep's feet,
There's plenty to eat on the street.'

'A can of milk, ladies, fresh today,
Cow's milk, sir, and eggs just laid,
Travelled from the country on a cart of hay
To bring these just for you.'

The costermonger and the common cry:
'What do you lack and will you buy?
I'll sing the news as you walk by
Along the streets of London.'

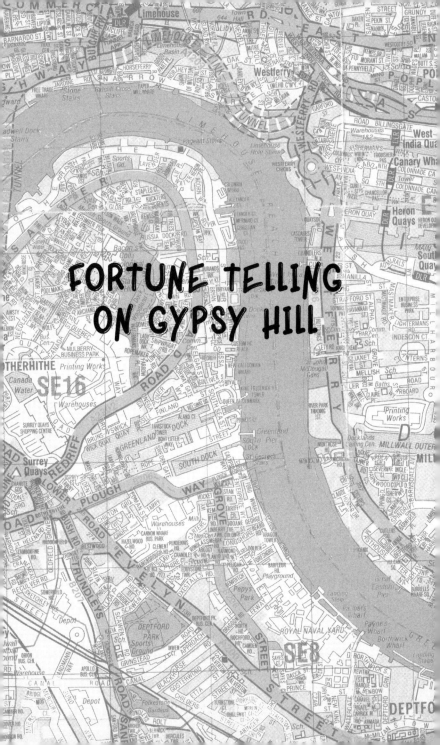

FORTUNE TELLING ON GYPSY HILL

Gypsy Hill got its name because gypsies, who were not allowed to camp in London, had to put up their tents and their wagons in the woodlands and on the open land outside the city. Well, London has grown so much that Gypsy Hill is no longer outside London but is now actually a part of it.

One famous gypsy who used to camp here was an old lady called Margaret Finch. She made a living by telling fortunes, which in the Romany – or Gypsy – language is known as 'dukkering'. She would look at people's hands and from the lines on their palms she would tell them what was happening in their life and what would happen in the future. She was so famous in her day that even Samuel Pepys wrote about her in his famous diary, because his own wife came to Gypsy Hill to have her fortune told.

Well, Margaret used to sit crouched down with her knees to her chest, smoking her pipe, with her dog at her side and she'd tell people's fortunes. She died at the age of 109 and, because she spent all her time

crouching down, she had to be buried in a square coffin as they couldn't straighten her legs to put her in a normal one. Now Margaret, like all gypsy folk, told stories sitting around the campfire, especially in winter when the darkness comes early. This little story would probably have been one she might have told. It tells us just how important observation is in fortune telling or 'dukkering':

You call us gypsies but *we* call ourselves Rom or Romany, and we've been travelling the world for hundreds of years. We started out in India and we've travelled through the Middle East, through Turkey, through France and through Spain. Well, those of us who ended up here in England survive by making baskets, wooden spoons and clothes pegs. We mend pots and pans and sometimes we tell fortunes because the Gorgios – the non-gypsies – love to know what life will bring them.

Now, we know that some people don't like us. But we think it's always better to be nice to people. We call them nice names, like 'my darling' and 'my dear' and even if they say horrible things, we try to be polite and cheerful and we try to see the good in everything. Well, one time there was a woman who didn't like her neighbour and would always be quarrelling with her. She was always very rude to her and called her nasty names. So this poor lady called over a gypsy woman whom she saw passing on the road, 'Oh please come here and I'll give you whatever I can if you'll just tell my fortune!'

'Well, of course, my dear,' she answered.

Just as the gypsy woman was coming over, she saw the neighbour make a really rude gesture to the woman and stick her tongue out at her. The gypsy noticed this and said, 'I see that this is a bad place for you to live. You are unhappy here because your neighbours are jealous of you. That is because you are a good woman and they don't like that, so they are rude and nasty to you.'

'That's amazing! You seem to know what's in my mind. What can I give you?

I'll give you whatever I can.' Then she gave her bread and cheese and fruit from the garden and said, 'You're so clever to know all that, please come back tomorrow when I shall have some money to give you.' The gypsy woman, who now had a long walk home to her camp outside the city, said she would come back the next day. She walked home happily, thinking of the good things she would share with her children.

Next day, as she was walking back into London, it started to rain very heavily, but she saw a cave and thought, 'I'll go in there and get dry.' As she entered the cave she saw that there was a lovely fire burning, and said to herself, 'Oh goodie! I can dry myself in the warmth of that fire.' As she got closer she noticed there was a group of young men sitting around the fire. There were twelve of them in all, and they all said together, 'Welcome grandmother, where are you going?' (She wasn't their grandmother at all, but in those days, that was a way of being polite.)

'Well, I was on my way back to the city but then it started to rain, so I came in here and found you, my dear children.'

'And why is it raining so hard? It's because it's March ... that awful month. Horrible rain and snow, miserable!'

'Oh, don't say that, my dears. March is the best month!' said the gypsy woman.

'Why is that?'

'Because March brings April ... and April brings the springtime, you see. So, without

March there would be no spring. And if there were no February there'd be no March, so you see, each month brings something good.'

By now it seemed that the rain had stopped and the gypsy woman said that she should go back to the camp to feed her hungry children. But before she left, the young men gave her a sack and told her to wait until she got home before she opened it. The old gypsy woman returned to her children and said, 'I didn't do any fortune telling today, but I found twelve lovely young men – twelve little angels – and they gave me this.'

'What's inside?' So all together they opened it – and what did they find? Golden coins! You see, the twelve young men were really the Twelve Months, and because the gypsy woman had something good to say about each month of the year and they liked that, she was rewarded with gold. Next day the weather was fine and the gypsy woman set out, as she'd promised, to the lady who had given her the bread and the cheese and the fruit from her garden.

On the way there she saw the rude neighbour. The woman was jealous and said, 'Whatever she gave you, I'll give you more. Just tell me what you want.'

'I don't want anything from you, as God has given me what I need.'

'And what did God give you?'

The gypsy woman told her everything about the cave and going in to dry off, and getting warm, and the young men, and everything.

Then the rude neighbour rushed to the cave of the Twelve Months and went in, pretending to be cold. The young men asked her what month it was, as she seemed so cold.

'It's March, of course. Everybody knows that! And it's the worst month of the lot. It's horrible and cold and miserable and wet!'

'So, what do you think of February?'

'Oh, that's even worse. It's terrible! Too much snow. Eughh!'

'Well, here, take this sack. But don't open it till you get home.'

The rude neighbour was delighted. She thought she had got a sack of gold too, like the gypsy woman had. It certainly was heavy! When she got home she said, 'Now let's see all those lovely golden coins. I'm so excited!' She opened the sack and out of it came a whole lot of snakes who ate everything in her house, including her.

Her neighbour now had no one calling her names and no one being nasty to her all day, and she said, 'That gypsy knew everything. She knew my neighbour was bad, so she did her magic on her.'

And that is why, ever since then, hundreds of years later, the people still say that the gypsies know everything! They'll certainly tell your fortune if you ask them – and you might be surprised at how much they seem to know about you!

The gypsy woman in this story is part of a people who have been travelling for hundreds of years. They are known by many names, but in England they call themselves Gypsy, Romany or Travellers. Each group has its own way of calling itself.

THE STRUGGLE
TO FEEL AT HOME

'Oh, the earth and the sea
and the sea and the sky,
If I only had wings
I would surely fly.
If I only had wings
and wishes came true,
I'd fly over the ocean to be with you.'

Duleep was thinking of a story his mother had told him when he was a little boy of ten and lived with her in Jammu, which is in India, where she was the Maharani Jind Kaur. It was a story of a bird with two heads and one body. The bird lived in a wavering forest of blue and green. It had two heads but only the one stomach. When one head drank the dew from the grass and bit a worm in half and ate it raw, the other head wasn't sure whether it was still hungry or not. Eating was a problem. With two heads everything was a problem. The bird had only two legs and two wings. One head might want to look at a snail feeling its way between the green stalks of grass, while the other head wanted to know which way a black beetle might be choosing to go. If one head wanted to fly, to open its wings and soar to the top of the trees in the blue and green forest, but the other head didn't, then this ended badly. The bird would flap its wings clumsily and get nowhere.

'I feel like that bird,' thought Duleep. 'My father was known as the Lion of the Punjab, but I feel nothing like that. Why am I here in London? Why is my mother not here?'

'I dream of the mountains, the Himalayas. I dream of our palace in Lahore. I dream my mother is here and that my father is not dead. Then I wake up and I am in this hotel in London. I hardly remember my father. I was tiny when he died and then everyone was making a huge fuss of me.

'I was a prince. I was the Maharajah of the Sikh empire with my mother ruling for me, and now I am just a rich Indian boy, living in a hotel in London with a guardian. I have none of my family here. If I am still a prince, then surely I can go where I want and see who I want, but I cannot. Everyone is so polite but I feel like a bird in a gilded cage. When I was only seven I had to bring the big diamond called the Koh-i-Noor, which means "the mountain of light", and present it to Queen Victoria. This diamond had always been in my family. When I was eleven there was a war and I signed papers that the British officials gave me, which gave my kingdom to them. I am still a prince, but a prince with no power. I wonder about my mother. I never hear from her. Is she still living in Jammu near the beautiful mountains? Why do I never hear from her?

'This hotel is called Claridge's. It is very new and expensive. I have people to look after me, I have plenty of money, clothes and food and of course that is nice. Dr John Login is my guardian. Dr John comes from Scotland and he has taught me about English ways and manners and how to be an English gentleman. I have good clothes and Dr John goes with me to visit the expensive shops in the Burlington Arcade. I ride horses in Hyde Park. I am invited to splendid houses and meet many ladies and gentlemen who are nice to me. Yet whenever I want to talk about my mother or to talk of India, then Dr John quickly begins to speak of something else. I was the Maharajah of the Sikh empire. What am I now?

'I feel like that bird with two heads. With one head I can see how lucky I am to be treated so well. I like the clothes and the food and the busy life of London, but I miss my

mother and I want to know why I cannot visit her. I want to know how she is. Why does no one want to talk about India? My head hurts and I have a bad feeling in my chest and stomach, like a swarm of moths fluttering to reach the light. One night I was looking out of the tall windows of my hotel. The stars were shivering small and white. Under a street lamp there was a small girl selling matches. She called out to all the gentlemen passing, 'A box o' matches, sir: 250 wax 'uns for a penny!' She stood calling out for a long time and did not sell many.

'In the morning there was another little girl about eight years old selling bunches of watercress. It was snowing but she was only dressed in a thin cotton gown, with a tattered shawl wrapped around her shoulders. When she walked, she shuffled along on the frozen ground. Her slippers were far too big for her and must have belonged to a grown-up.

'I am confused: Dr John said England was the best place to live, yet here in London, the capital of this country, little children stand barefoot in the dirty streets and earn only pennies, while rich people wear silks and satins and fine leather shoes. The rich people ride in carriages and pass the poor children by without a glance. In India this also happens.

'I have trouble sleeping. Every night, the shadows creep from the corners of my room and climb onto the end of my large bed. I have such real dreams. My dreams feel more real to me than my life when I am awake. When Dr John lights the lamp early in the winter mornings, the room is still full of sleep. I feel I am waiting for something to happen. Either my mother will arrive or someone will explain why she isn't coming. Why does no one explain anything? I am not a child. I am fifteen and anyway, a child's feelings are every bit as big as a grown-up's.

'I wonder how the children who sell matches and watercress in the streets feel about living in London. Maybe they feel angry in their hearts because no one is looking after them properly, but maybe they also get to go where they want. Dr John doesn't want me to speak to the children. I am not sure I want to either. They are very dirty and I might catch a disease, but I watch them from the windows of my room.

'One morning Dr John pulled back the curtains and I wondered if there had been a flood. There were so many big puddles. The sun came out and the cold blue sky and white clouds were reflected in the puddles. It looked as though the sky was on the ground. It seemed all the world was upside down. I thought to myself, "Well, my world is upside down, so I just might as well have some fun." I have decided that as I am here in London I will make the best of it. I'll ride in Hyde Park. I will buy some new clothes. I will ask to be presented to Queen Victoria.'

Duleep became a favourite of Queen Victoria and was often at the palace. Queen Victoria became godmother to three of Duleep's children. He did see his mother eight years later, in Calcutta when he was twenty-three years old. He brought her back to England, and for the last two years of her life she told him more of his Sikh heritage and of the empire which once had been his to rule. One of the addresses in England that Duleep lived at was 53 Holland Park, London W11.

THE SWEEP'S SONG

'I wish,' said the barefoot boy,
covered in soot and grime,
'that my eyes glowed red,
that I lived in a hole
like a rat, that would be fine;
for a rat can come and go,
has the waterside to roam
and any hole he finds in the ground
he turns into a home.'

'I wish,' said the barefoot boy,
covered in soot and grime,
'that my blood ran cold,
that I swam in the tide
like a fish, that would be fine;
for a fish can swim unseen
and with the herring play,
have food and drink enough,
be free both night and day.'

'I wish,' said the barefoot boy,
covered in soot and grime,
'that my arms were wings,
that I flew in the sky
like a bird, that would be fine;
for a bird has roofs and trees,
the whole sky is his own,
he can perch on a ledge or the
branch of a tree
and that will be
his home.'

Most boys who worked for a chimney sweep came from the workhouse. There was nobody to care for them and some of the masters treated them very badly. The boys had to climb up inside the chimneys and clear the soot that had not come away with the brushes. It was dirty and dangerous work.

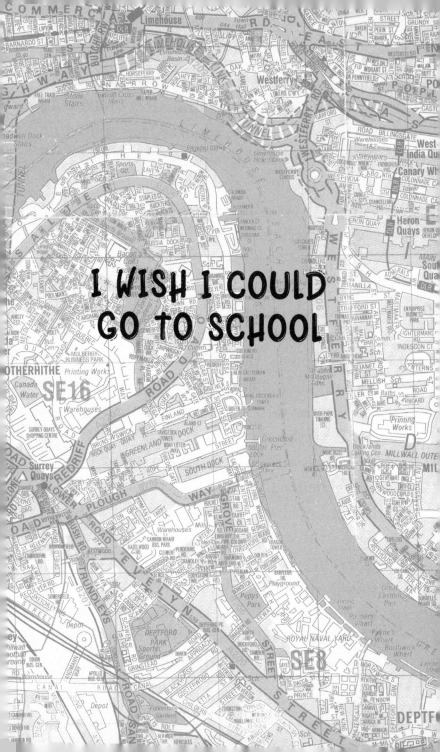

The snow had begun in the evening and had been heaping streets and alleys busily all night with a frozen silence, deep and white. Little Liza MacDonald was eight years old and had to leave the warm bed she shared with her two little sisters and make her way to Farringdon Market to buy a bundle of watercress that she could divide up into small bunches and sell in the streets. It was five o'clock in the morning and already the snow was churned up by carriage wheels and horses' hooves, pushed aside by the crossing sweepers and dirtied with horse dung.

Liza had thin slippers that were too big for her. They had belonged to her mother. Her father was a bricklayer's labourer, which meant he fetched and carried the bricks and mortar for the bricklayer so that the bricklayer did not have to stop working to fetch them himself. It was heavy work and badly paid and he only found work a couple of days a week, so Liza worked too, otherwise there would not be enough to pay the rent on their one room and there would be no food to eat.

Liza's mother had died one cold winter when Liza was six years old. Liza's father and mother were born in Scotland and had come to London to find work. They had one room in a house shared with five other families.

Last night the sun had set cherry red; Liza's mother had always said that when the sun set as red as that, it meant snow would fall soon and she was right. She had been right about so many things. There had been a baby, a baby boy. Liza remembered him lying on Mother and Father's bed. He lay there raging, small and red, but he didn't live and neither did Mother.

Liza thought of her mother every day and she also remembered her mother saying, 'It's no use crying.' Liza had cried, though, but now she was determined that she would make a better life for herself and help Father make a better life for her little sisters. 'Perhaps today,' Liza thought, 'I will be lucky, like I was last Wednesday when I earnt one shilling and sixpence. That was enough to buy a penny loaf every single day and have money over. Wednesday is my lucky day.

The old rhyme that Mother taught me says that Wednesday's child is full of woe but I was born on a Wednesday and I often earn good money on a Wednesday.'

Liza's mother and father had gone to Sunday school when they were children and had learnt to read and write a little. Liza's mother had taught Liza how to read but not as well as she would like to. She couldn't read long words and she had very little chance to practise her writing. She wanted to go to school but that wasn't easy. School cost money and she had to work. Liza said to herself, 'I will go to school somehow: after all, the sun shines on the rich and the poor, on the palaces and on the houses where *we* live with a family in every room.'

Sometimes there were old newspapers left on the street and Liza had read that the Prime Minister was a man called William Gladstone and he wanted all the people to learn to read and write – and if the Prime Minister thought that, then there must be a way.

When Liza was on the streets trying to sell her bunches of watercress, she listened carefully to the bits of conversation she heard between the ladies and gentlemen that passed by. After all, it was no crime to listen. One day a lady and gentleman were walking by; they were not dressed as fancy as many but neither were they poor.

The lady was saying to the man, 'But Andrew, I would like to help at the ragged school. I can teach the girls to read and write and other useful things.'

Before she could stop herself, Liza spoke up. 'Sorry, Ma'am, I couldn't help hearing what you said. Please, Ma'am, what is a ragged school?'

The lady turned around. She had a kind face and the man didn't look cross. She told Liza that a ragged school was one for children who couldn't afford to pay for lessons.

'Where is it, Ma'am?' said Liza. 'I would like to go there.'

'We have a new building on Saffron Hill. Lord Shaftesbury laid the first stone himself two years ago. Have you not seen it?'

Liza answered, 'I have seen it, Ma'am, but I didn't think the likes of me could go there. It looks a very fine place.'

'It is now,' said the lady, 'but when the school started in Field Lane it was very shabby and very hard to run a school there. We have been very lucky: some very important people support us and we have been given money to build this new school. Tell me where you live, child, and I will go and speak to your parents.'

'My mother is dead, Ma'am, but my father will speak with you. I am sure he will let me come, as long as I can work as well. We do need the money. My mother would be very happy to know that I was learning to read and write better than I do.'

The lady told Liza that her name was Miss Beatrice and the gentleman was Mr Andrew. Liza told her that she lived with her father and two little sisters near Saffron Hill but she wasn't sure that a lady would like to visit, as there were some very dirty alleys and it could be quite rough. But Miss Beatrice said she would be fine and there was something about the way she said it that meant Liza believed her.

Miss Beatrice and Mr Andrew bought all of Liza's bunches of watercress, a whole shilling's worth, and promised they would see her soon. They went on their way and Liza hugged herself. She thought, 'My mother would be so pleased and she would have given me a hug.'

Then soon after Miss Beatrice and Mr Andrew visited Liza's father and he was very pleased to see how they were interested in helping Liza get on in life. He asked if her little sisters could also come along. They said they had a special room for the little ones and they could come too.

Liza went to visit the very next day, thinking, 'I just know it will be like heaven to be in school. It was a Wednesday when I met Miss Beatrice and Mr Andrew and I am not full of woe. Maybe I am a little bit of all the days of the week.'

Monday's child is fair of face.
'Well, I think I look all right.'

Tuesday's child is full of grace.
'Well, I am not clumsy and I do say my prayers.'

Wednesday's child is full of woe.
'Well, I will always miss Mother.'

Thursday's child has far to go.
'Well, I think now I can go to school, I will go far.'

Friday's child is loving and giving.
*'Well, I loved my mother. I love my father and
little sisters and I give Father the money I earn.'*

Saturday's child works hard for their living.
'Well, I certainly do.'

But the child that is born on the Sabbath day
is bonny and blithe and good all day.
*'Well, as I said before, I think I look all right
and I feel very happy now and Father tells me I
am a good girl.'*

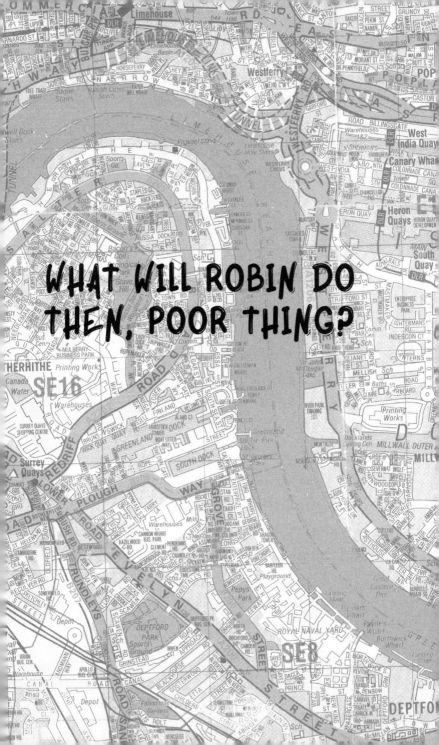

The little bird has whistled
from the top of the holly tree,
his breast as red as the berry,
a merry little bird is he.
He's bold and bright and
he throws his song over the garden wall,
where another little bird,
from the top of a bush, answers his call.
The ground is white with a hard frost,
The sun drops from the sky,
the twigs are as bare as a witch's broom
but the small birds stay on high.
Whistle for whistle 'til the first star blinks,
Whistle 'til the grey dusk falls,
only then with a flicker and a dart
do they leave their branches tall.

I was the little one in the bed with my two big sisters, but I was not going to roll over and fall out. It was far too cold to want to get out of bed. It was February in the year 1895 and the Grand Surrey Canal was frozen solid. The winter had been so cold that the Thames was blocked in places by great ice floes.

My father had work trying to break up the ice on the canal so the supplies of coal could get through to the gas company's site on the Old Kent Road. The coal was heaped onto barges with tugs pulling them, but they were stuck fast in the ice. Everyone needed coal for the fires to keep houses warm, for the steam trains to run, for the factories to work. Coal was really important. Father would come home frozen to the bone and so tired that we helped pull off his boots and Mother would

rub his feet until he was able to feel them again. When I got up I would wear all the clothes I had, and Mother would wrap me round in an old shawl, criss-crossed at the front and pinned at the back.

We lived in Culling Road, Bermondsey. We had lived there all my life and much longer than that. My grandparents came from Munster in Ireland forty years before and we all lived in this little house: Grandpa, Grandma, Mother, Father and we three sisters.

Grandpa and Grandma had a room and Mother and Father had a room and we three sisters shared a room and a big bed. We also had a kitchen big enough to sit down in and for all of us to sit around the table. The kitchen range kept the whole house warm and we kept it burning night and day that winter so we would not freeze to death indoors. I know we were very lucky. I had friends whose whole family lived in one room: cooked, ate, washed and slept all in the same room.

We were lucky because Father was strong and mostly had work and Mother cleaned the priest's house. Grandma could sew and would keep our few clothes looking decent. As Mother worked it meant that I and my two sisters, Maggie and Catherine, had to keep the house clean and see that Grandpa was looked after, as he was not that well.

One day in the middle of that freezing winter, I decided to go out. I liked the frosty air, I liked seeing my breath floating out in front of me. I liked to see the icicles hanging from the roofs and I liked to try to crack the milky ice that covered the puddles, with my boots. I went towards the river. There were market gardens on the way and maybe not all the turnips that were still in the ground were frozen and I could dig up one or two to go into the stew pot. There were hedgerows which in late summer and autumn were covered with blackberries. Now the bare twigs and branches were white with frost. I wondered what happened to all the little birds that lived in those bushes. The hedgerows were home to so many small birds and now all was white and silent.

I tied the shawl around my head and shoulders more tightly. I hadn't gone a few yards when I saw a little robin hunched in a corner of the yard we shared with the other little houses. I picked it up; it was cold, but still living. I stood warming it in both my hands and then went back indoors with it still cupped in my hands, its little beak opening and closing, but making no sound.

Mother saw me straight away and said, 'Annie, take that bird outside. Indoors is no place for it.'

'But Mother,' I said, 'it will die outside. We can look after it.'

Then Grandma spoke up: 'Mary,' she said – that was my mother's name. 'Sure you can't ask the child to take that bird back out. It is one of God's creatures and Annie knows the story as well as you do about how the robin came to have its red breast. I have told it to you often enough.'

Mother sighed and agreed that I could keep the robin and look after it indoors.

Here is the story Grandma told me:

Once there was a boy and his father who had been turned out of their home by the landlord and chased off their own land. It was a bitter winter and they could find no place to sleep. The boy was footsore and nearly dead with tiredness, so the father made a bed for them both as best he could among the bushes. He collected dry leaves, twigs and dead branches to make a fire. They slept close to the fire to keep warm and hoped the fire would frighten away any hungry beasts.

They were both so tired that they fell into a deep sleep. The fire burned brightly and soon the branches were smouldering embers among a heap of grey ash. A starving wolf who had been watching from the edge of the wood came closer and closer. The wolf intended to kill and eat both the man and the boy. A robin was also watching from the depths of the bush. This small, brave, brown bird flew closer to the fire, fanning the embers with its little wings until they burst into flame.

The little bird did not stop even when the heat burned its breast. The flames rose higher, the crackling of the fire woke the father who chased away the wolf with a burning stick and then he built up the fire again. The little robin's breast was now red and has always been so to this day.

'It's a bonny, brave bird,' said Grandma. 'You wouldn't put it outside to die.' That was in February and now it is March. It is beginning to get warmer and soon I know my robin will want to go outside and begin building its nest in the hedgerow, but for now he is perched on the end of my bed and I will feed him little bits of my breakfast.

The north wind doth blow
There will be snow
And what will robin do then, poor thing?
He'll sit in a barn and keep himself warm
And hide his head under his wing,
Poor thing.

Light as thistledown my tail.
My road, my trail,
the trunks of trees.
None but I know how
to balance both on twig and bough.
Eyes bright as buttons,
tiny paws,
tufted ears
and nibbling jaws.

Hello, my name is Frisk. I am a red squirrel and you can find me in Kensington Gardens. I am carved into the pedestal of the statue of Peter Pan which is next to the Long Water. Peter Pan is the boy who never grew up. The man who wrote the story of Peter Pan was J.M. Barrie, and he lived near these gardens. The statue appeared in the gardens on 1 May 1912, as if by magic. It had been put there secretly in the middle of the night. The statue is as magical as the story.

What you will never see is that when the sun goes down over the Long Water, over the Flower Walk, over the Sunken Gardens and over the Albert Memorial, then I come alive again, along with the rabbits, the mice and the Fairy Folk that live in the Elfin Oak.

You may be able to hear the Fairy Folk singing in small high voices:

'*We'll come out,*
  when twilight to moonlight turns.
  When the owl hoots from the park,
  when the fox slides,

a slick red shadow in the dark,
then we'll come out.'

I was the last red squirrel in Kensington Gardens. That was a long time ago, nearly 100 years ago. All the other red squirrels moved to Scotland but I could not bear to leave the gardens. I was an old squirrel by then and I decided I was too old to move away from all that I knew.

There were children who used to bring me nuts to eat. I liked to run up to them. They would hold out a nut on the palm of their hand and I would quickly take it. The children loved me. There are still children in the gardens. They wear different clothes nowadays. One hundred years ago the girls all wore dresses and the boys often wore little sailor suits. In the summer they would play with spinning tops and hoops. Many of the children came from the big houses on the Bayswater Road and they were brought to the gardens by their childminders, who were called nannies.

There was plenty to eat.

There were oak trees from which I collected acorns. There were sweet chestnut trees and I stored the chestnuts in many different hiding places. Some of the acorns and chestnuts which I buried in the ground have grown into trees. Many of the trees I knew as a young squirrel are still in the gardens. Come, visit and see for yourself. There are oak trees that are 160 years old. There are graceful silver birch, London plane, horse chestnut and delicious cherry and crab apple trees.

I lived in a hollow oak and sadly that old tree has now gone. It fell in the great storm of 1973. I had no need of it by then. I was already part of the Peter Pan statue.

But I have a story to tell you from the time when I was a squirrel with a beating heart:

My oak tree was near the South Flower Walk where the nursemaids and nannies used to walk with the children they looked after. It was a lovely sparkly May morning and I was sorting out my dray, putting some new oak leaves on the floor, scolding the other creatures that lived in the tree, telling them to keep out of my home. Did you know that beetles and spiders live in the bark of trees? There was one really cheeky spider that would hang on a silken thread just in front of my door.

Then I heard children spinning their hoops along the path and their nanny was calling after them to come back. I looked out and saw that the nanny was limping and could not keep up with the children.

She called after them time and again, 'Beatrice, Osbert, come back. Mama has told you to stay with me. Come back and sit with me under this lovely tree and I will tell you a story.'

The two children came running back, chanting, 'Story, story, let it come, let it go,' and then sat down with their nanny.

Nanny began by saying, 'Have you heard of Peter the wild boy who used to walk around in these gardens?'

'No,' said the two children, 'where is he now? Can we see him?'

'No,' said Nanny, 'you can't see him now. He is dead a long time ago, nearly 300 years ago. King George the First brought him to England. King George was in Germany and he was out hunting in the forest near the town of Hamelin. Yes, the same place where the Pied Piper got rid of all the rats. It was in the forest he came across this boy of about nine years of age. The boy ran on all fours and he couldn't speak but made the sounds of different creatures of the forest. He fed himself on berries and fruits that grew in the forest. King George brought him to Kensington Palace and hired tutors to teach the boy, but he never learnt to speak. There is a painting in Kensington Palace with the boy Peter in it. In the painting he is wearing a green coat and is holding oak leaves and acorns.'

'Is that really true?' said the children. 'How could he live in a forest all by himself?'

'Well,' said Nanny, 'there is a story from Spain, the country where I was born, that might explain how a boy like Peter came to be living on his own in a forest.'

'Tell us the story, please,' said the children.

Nanny began and I settled down to listen:

There was once a husband and wife who badly wanted a child. They had a little house and a small garden, where the wife grew vegetables. The husband made wooden toys and furniture with wood from the forest: they sold these and had all they wanted, except that they didn't have a child.

One day the wife told her husband that their wish had come true. She was expecting a baby. They were both so happy and busy getting everything ready for the baby. The man made a wooden cradle and a little chair for the baby to sit in when it got bigger. He made a wooden rattle and small wooden bricks. The woman sewed the prettiest clothes and knitted little jumpers and shawls.

The baby was born, a little boy, and like all babies do he cried as soon as he opened his eyes. He was a strong and healthy baby and he

grew quickly. Soon he was crawling and then walking unsteadily around the small kitchen holding on to the chairs. The man made him a little cart to push around the kitchen.

He grew into a strong little boy. Perhaps he didn't know his own strength, because soon most of the toys that his father had made for him were broken. He liked to climb on to the table and to go too near the fire. He liked to do everything that his parents didn't want him to do. Neither did he sleep very much and soon both parents were looking old and tired and worried.

One day the woman said to the man, 'Oh why did we want a child so much?

Look what has become of us. We are fading away with worry and too little sleep.'

'I feel the same way,' said the man. 'Let us take him to the forest and leave him there.'

And that is what they did. They took the little boy to the forest and crept away home while the boy was climbing a tree.

When he came down from the tree and saw that his mother and father were nowhere to be seen, he began to cry. The sun was setting and he was afraid and he was hungry. Then he spotted a large nut on the forest floor. He had never seen a nut like it. He had watched squirrels bury nuts so he did the same. While he was digging a hole in the earth he was saying to himself, 'I wish I had something to eat and somewhere safe to sleep. I am afraid that there may be wild beasts in the forest.'

The nut was now hidden under the earth but no sooner was it buried than it began to grow. A small green shoot appeared above the earth, then grew quickly into a strong trunk that sprouted branches, which put out twigs – and then leaves and fruits appeared.

What wonderful fruits. All shapes and sizes, all colours and scents. Then this beautiful tree grew small thick branches like a ladder. When the boy climbed up into the shelter of the rustling leaves, on the topmost branches he found a huge nest that he curled up into, taking with him some of the fruit to eat.

He slept, and when asleep, he dreamed of the tree. He could see the roots stretching out and down. He saw a badger burrowing deep to make his bed and sleep. He saw the tiny creatures living in the rough and rutted bark. He saw spiders hanging from silken threads. He saw birds roosting in the branches. He felt safe and looked after. The tree was alive and had a heart and he was just another of the creatures that found shelter there.

The days passed and the boy ate the fruits and watched the birds and creatures of the forest. He missed his mother and his father. He wished he could hear his mother sing him a lullaby once more. No sooner had he wished it than a light wind rustled the leaves and he was rocked and sung to sleep. He missed his

father's strong arms around him and then he found a place to sit in the tree where he was held snugly on both sides by the branches and he was comforted.

Meanwhile the man and woman were feeling very bad. They did not sleep well and when they did, they had nightmares. They had no appetite and grew thin and worn.

'What have we done, husband?' asked the wife. 'How shall we ever be forgiven for doing such a terrible thing?'

The man said, 'We must go back to the forest and find him. We have done wrong and we will never have peace until we try to put it right.'

They set out on the path towards the forest. They made for the place where they had left the boy. The forest seemed to fall silent. They heard nothing but their own breathing and the beating of their hearts. The man and woman felt that there were eyes watching them. They came to the clearing where they had left him and to the tree that he had been climbing. Now next to that tree was this amazing tree. A tree that grew all kinds of fruit. A tree where the wind sang in the branches when everywhere else in the forest was silent. They looked up and up to the topmost branches and there looking down at them was their boy. He was well, he was smiling and he climbed down to his mother and father.

'The tree looked after me,' he said. The man and woman got down on to their knees and thanked the tree for looking after their son and they promised that they would all visit the tree every month and bring the tree a gift. They did just that and if you ever come across a tree with small gifts of ribbons and ornaments tied to its branches you will have found the tree in this story, or maybe another very like it.

The children had snuggled up to their nanny and now the sun was setting over the Flower Walk. Well, when I heard that story I thought how it was that the trees looked after all life and that the boy that King George brought to England, Wild Peter, may have climbed into the same oak tree that I am now living in. I thought about the story and went to sleep.

What happened next? I don't really know but when I woke up I was not in the oak tree. I was part of the Peter Pan statue. A kind of magic happened. I fell asleep listening to the story of Wild Peter who had played in the gardens 300 years ago and now I was part of the magical statue of another Peter: Peter Pan. Please do come and visit me.

Frisk, the red squirrel.

For hundreds of years the people living in the East End of London have been called Cockneys. No one knows exactly why they were called this, but what people do know is that many Cockneys had a special way of speaking – it's called rhyming slang. This means that, instead of saying words as we all know them, you use a couple of words that rhyme with the word you mean. So instead of saying 'Going up the stairs' you would say 'Going up the apples and pears'; 'Go to bed' is 'Go to me Uncle Ned', and so on. This poem shows more of the fun rhyming expressions that Cockneys had for things that we see every day.

Adam and Eve it – don't believe it;
Skin and blister – she's my sister;
Oh, oh, life's so fine, life's so fine, it blows my
mind – SAY IT [repeat];
Daisy roots – they're my boots;
Plates of meat – they're my feet.

Chorus

Mince pies – they're my eyes;
Butcher's hook – take a look.

Chorus

Loaf of bread – that's my head;
Barnet fair – that's my hair.

Chorus

Uncle Bert – that's my shirt;
Weasel and stoat – that's my coat.

Chorus

Jam jar – that's my car;
Rub a dub dub – that's the pub.

Chorus

Scapa Flow – let's go;
Alligator – see you later.

Chorus

I want to tell you the story of how my family became Londoners. My grandfather was a dental technician in Berlin before the war. He was a partner in a dental laboratory where they make things like false teeth and crowns and bridges and all those things that dentists need.

Now, in a dental laboratory in those days – and probably even today – what you have to do is take great care with the sweepings from the floor. Every night they would carefully sweep the laboratory floor and keep what they swept up. Then they would put it in a jar and every couple of weeks they would take the dust and roll it between a cigarette paper and burn off the rubbish. And what was left was this dirty-looking metal stuff. But it wasn't just dirt; it wasn't just any old metal; it was gold. Gold that had been left over from filing down gold caps and crowns that were used to repair teeth.

Well, my grandfather was a proud German, he fought in the First World War, but he was also a Jew. And things became very difficult for Jews after Hitler and his horrible Nazi party came to power. There were all sorts of rules stopping Jews from working, from going to school and from mixing with people who weren't Jewish. It eventually reached the point where my grandfather couldn't even sleep at home. He had to move from friend's place to friend's place each night because there was the danger of him being arrested and sent away to a big prison, called a concentration camp.

My father, who was called Simon, couldn't even play out on the streets with the other children. They finally decided they should leave the country and go to London where my grandmother had family. My grandfather applied for a permit and it took some time, and during that time they thought about what they could take out of the country. But the law was that German Jews could only take a few of their personal possessions with them: the clothes that they had, a small amount of money, a hundred Reichsmarks, and personal jewellery that had been in the family since before 1933 when Hitler came to power.

My grandfather took the gold that he had collected over the years to a man who cast them into two gold rings – signet rings – which meant that they had the initials of my grandfather on one of them and my grandmother's on the other. He was trying to create something that looked like it was obviously personal, these rings with their initials on them, so that they could keep hold of something of value from what they owned. It was important to have something and these gold rings meant they could take something valuable with them.

The Nazis were very keen to take as much from these unfortunate Jewish people as they could get from them. Before they could plan to leave the country, they had to take the rings to a government office so that they could get a piece of paper which would say exactly what they were taking out of the country. The rings were then put into envelopes and sealed with the Nazi symbol of the swastika so that they wouldn't be able to open the envelopes and put something else in.

In 1939 the time finally came when they had a permit to leave and the family packed up the few possessions they were allowed to take with them, along with the gold rings in those sealed envelopes marked with the Nazi swastika. The train left Berlin and they travelled nervously through the German countryside, hoping that all would go well and that they wouldn't be stopped and sent back. The train eventually arrived at the border with Holland.

It came to a shuddering halt and everybody in the carriage became anxious as they were ordered off the train and, in turn, each member of the family was interrogated on their own. First my grandfather and then my grandmother and then Simon, who was only nine years old.

The guards were very jokey with him, as though they were trying to trick him into saying something that he shouldn't have been saying about what they were carrying.

'So, little man, where are you going to?'

'We are going to London.'

'Oh, London is it? And where will you be staying in London?'

'We are staying with my mother's family.'

'And what are you carrying with you?'

'Just our clothes and a little money and two gold rings.'

'Gold rings, eh? How long have these gold rings been in your family?'

They were still very jokey with him, as if they were trying to trick him into saying something wrong. Well, now the boy was worried – because if he told the truth they would be arrested and sent back to Berlin and this would be very dangerous for them. But his mother had always told him that he should never tell lies, because if you tell lies you will always be found out.

The guard again said, 'Come on. How long have these gold rings been in your family?' But at this point Simon said something that *was* true. Because he was always in a world of his own, a world full of stories and daydreams, he often couldn't remember what he was doing last week, and so he said, 'Er, as long as I can remember.'

'As long as you can remember? So, tell me, how old are you?'

'I'm nine years old.'

The guard thought, 'It's now 1939, so he was born in 1930, so that must mean they've had them before Hitler became our leader,' and then said, 'Oh well in that case, you can go. Get back on the train!'

The family were allowed back on the train and the train passed through the border. The moment the train had crossed the border into Holland a sense of relief passed through the whole carriage. Simon's mother and father took the gold rings out of the sealed envelopes and put them on their fingers. The train then went to the coast of Holland

and to the harbour, where the train went on to a boat and eventually they arrived at Liverpool Street station in London, where my grandmother's family were waiting to meet them.

It was lucky for the family that they did manage to get through the border that day. Other members of the family who stayed behind in Germany didn't survive; they were sent to concentration camps where they died. And it was lucky for me too, or I wouldn't be here today to tell you this story and to show you this gold ring.

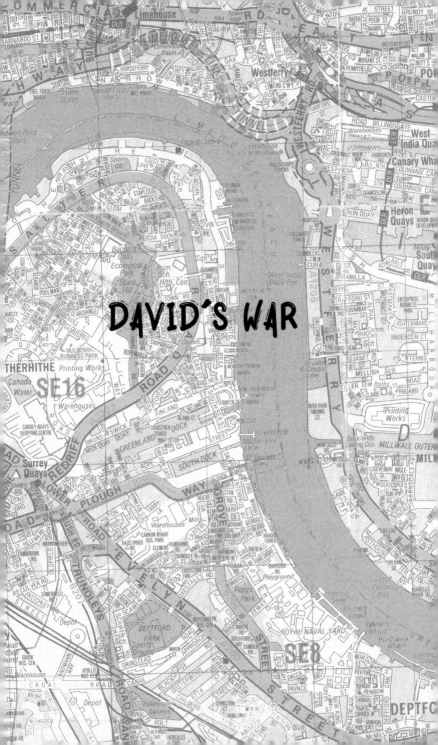

People thought that London would be a very dangerous place for children in the war that had just been declared and there was a mass transportation of children to the countryside. It was called 'evacuation' and was to make sure that they would be safe from the bombs that everyone expected would be dropped on the city by enemy planes. David found himself on a train at Waterloo station with hundreds of other children from London. He had a label pinned to his blazer, with his name and destination written on it. 'I'm just like a parcel being sent away to another place,' he thought.

Then he felt his little sister, Lily, squeezing and holding tightly to his hand. She had her own label pinned to her little blue jacket. His mother, along with all the other London mothers, was fighting back tears and they sadly waved their children goodbye as the train pulled out from the platform.

This was the beginning of September 1939 and no one knew how long they would be away from their parents. It was all for

their safety, they'd said, but by the time the train pulled into the little country station in Devon, David and Lily were feeling very hungry, very tired, and not sure if they were feeling safe at all.

Even though David was almost ten, he could feel the tears welling up in his eyes. He knew other boys at school would often laugh if they saw a boy crying, but when he looked around, many of the other boys looked as if they were going to burst into tears too. Then he remembered that he had to make sure that he and Lily must not get separated and he soon forgot about being scared. He put his arm around her, saying that everything would be all right.

He looked around the village hall where all the children from London had been lined up, waiting to be chosen by a host family. A lady with rosy cheeks and a big smile was walking over to them, saying, 'I'll take these two, they look so frightened, poor little nippers.' This was Mrs Scattergood, who tried her hardest to make them welcome on the farm where she lived with Tobias, her husband. She cooked lovely meals and delicious apple pies right out of their own orchard. But it just wasn't home. The children at school talked funny and called the London evacuees 'vacs' or 'Cockney titches'. And though every day Lily loved seeing the sheep, chickens, goats and cows, every night she cried for her mum.

By the time Christmas was coming close, everyone in London was saying, 'Why should our children be living with strangers, unhappy and far away from us, when no bombs have been dropped? Our children should be home with us to celebrate Christmas together.' Their dad then came one weekend to take his children back and they were all waved off at the station by lovely, smiley Mrs Scattergood and Tobias. They arrived back in London and when they saw the four huge gas holders of Stepney Gasworks, towering above all the houses, they knew they were well and truly home and they were happy.

But things in London had changed quite a lot in this war that had been going on now for more than three months. And, because there had been no bombing yet, they called it a 'phony war'. Anyway, one of the first changes that David noticed was the funny little shed things that seemed to be in everyone's back garden. His dad explained that they were Anderson shelters, in case of air raids. They were metal bomb shelters built of corrugated iron sheets and were half buried in the garden and then covered with soil. People thought this would be safer than staying in the house, if bombs were falling.

He also noticed that the kerbs on the pavements were painted with white lines. 'That's because of the blackout,' said his dad. 'All street lighting is switched off at night and people have to cover their windows with heavy black material to stop any glimmer of light shining through. With everything all dark down here, the enemy planes won't see

where the houses and factories are to drop their bombs on.' But people kept losing their way and falling into the road and there were many more traffic accidents at night. The white lines were meant to help.

What David and Lily really noticed was that there was less food to eat in London than in Devon. On the farm, Mrs Scattergood had fed them scrumptious fresh food and lots of it, but with the rationing each person was allowed only one egg a week, a few ounces of margarine, some bread, a little meat and not much sugar. This was so that the food could be shared out equally for all the people, because the ships that brought the food to our country couldn't sail the seas safely. Many of them had been sunk by enemy submarines.

Because the whole country was now at war, women like his mum were doing all sorts of jobs that only men had done before. They were driving trains and buses, lorries and ambulances, and they were working in factories and delivering letters. His mother was making parts for war planes in a factory that was hidden in the tunnels of a disused underground station. All of this was so the men could be free to go and join the fighting forces needed in a war.

But David's dad didn't go to fight because he had a very important job. He worked at the gasworks making gas for people to heat their homes and cook their food and so that the factories had power to do their work. The gas had to be stored in huge drums that were as big as half a football field and as high as four houses. They were called gasometers.

Everyone knew that if a gasometer was hit by bombs it could explode and do terrible damage, even demolish all the houses around it. All the workers at the gasworks had to take it in turn to be on 'firewatch'. This meant staying up all night and standing on top of the gasometer to check for any firebombs landing. If any landed they would have to put them out quickly before they had a chance to burst into flames and start a major fire.

But these bombing raids that everyone expected and that caused children to be sent away were just not happening. That's why people brought their children back from evacuation. The summer that followed was just like any summer in peacetime and in early September 1940 the weather was beautiful and still really hot. The sun shone all day and after school all the children were having a great time playing in the park, not far from the gasworks.

Then, all of a sudden one day after tea, everything changed. They heard the wailing sound of an air-raid siren and everyone knew what to do. Dad was at work, so Mum rushed the children into the little cramped Anderson shelter in the back garden. Outside it, David's job had been to make sure there were buckets filled with sand and filled with water in case a stray firebomb were to land nearby. They could hear their neighbours in the next gardens doing the same and they could sense everyone's fear.

Then they heard the awful whistling sound of bombs falling, then the heavy thud of bursting explosions and the terrifying rumble of the ground shaking underneath them. Mum had taken blankets and flasks of tea and a tin of biscuits. But, huddled in the damp-smelling and cramped shelter, nobody could eat a thing and nobody slept a wink.

Almost every single night for the next few months the enemy bombers would fly over London and drop their bombs. The big fear was a direct hit with a high-explosive bomb, but mostly clusters of small firebombs were dropped which, if not put out quickly, could start a huge firestorm. Although they hated it, they were getting used to the nights in the cold, damp air-raid shelter. But the worst nights were when Dad had his firewatch duty on top of the gasometers.

They thought of him high up on the gasometers with all the firebombs coming down in clusters. Then one night, just after Christmas, up there, so high above Stepney, their dad could see the docks of London going up in flames. Wave after wave of bombers dropped hundreds of bombs and

the warehouses, filled with timber, flour and sugar, burst into flames that went high into the sky. Dad could see that this was the biggest raid so far and as he looked west he could see St Paul's Cathedral completely surrounded by flames.

But then, suddenly, his eye was caught by a flash of light near to him. It was a firebomb! There were flames! But the phosphorous – like the stuff at the end of a match – hadn't gone off yet, so he had to be quick with the wet blanket that he always had ready. He just managed to put it out before it could start a fire and he was thinking how lucky he'd been, but he missed seeing that another had landed behind him. As he turned he saw the phosphorus ignite just like a big match being struck. By the time he got to it he could see that a hole was burning in the gasometer's steel plating with a five-foot-high flame!

He had to think fast. He quickly grabbed one of the buckets of wet clay that were ready by the handrail of the gasometer and upturned it over the flame. It worked! The wet clay filled the hole and extinguished the flame in moments. If he hadn't put it out and if air had got into the gasometer, there would have been the biggest explosion, demolishing the whole of the gasworks and all the buildings around it.

Next morning, after the night that people called the Second Great Fire of London, Dad came to the backyard shelter to see if his family was all right. He was tired, dirty and his eyebrows were singed from the fire. 'Come on, then!' he said. 'Let's go into the house and have breakfast, I don't want to be late for work.' They all hugged each other and went into the house, smelling the strong smell of burning in the air that was usual after a raid.

As David and Lily walked to school they could see the big black clouds of smoke coming from over the docks. The school playground was covered in broken glass that had been blasted out of the classroom windows. There were buildings around without roofs and the streets were filled with rubble from the bombed houses. But David was proud, and he never forgot just what a hero his dad had been in the Second World War.

The war did eventually come to an end and David, now many years later, is an old man. The gasworks are now gone but this old man, who was just a boy in those terrible times of war, is still living in the area in a block of flats which is called 'Firewatch Court', in memory of the men of the gasworks, including his dad, who saved the lives of so many people of Stepney in the East End of London.

THE CHILDREN IN THE MAGNOLIA TREE

Farah loves telling stories and, as she has spent lots of her time in the East End of London, she likes telling stories of a very famous street there which is called Brick Lane. She tells stories of the life on the street, of the colourful street markets, the shops and cafés and of all the different people who have come to live there over all the centuries of London's history.

Because Brick Lane is so close to the old docks of London, the people, coming off the ships that landed at London docks, settled very close to where they had arrived, and that was on Brick Lane. In the 1600s French people called Huguenots came here to become new Londoners. Then there were the Irish and the Jewish people, Somali families from East Africa and Farah's own people, those from Bangladesh. All of these people with their different languages, delicious foods, lovely music and customs came to Brick Lane and became Londoners, just like Farah.

Farah has loved poems and stories ever since she was a little girl, so as well as telling stories, she started writing them down and became a writer and a poet. She has written her stories and poems in books and newspapers both in Britain and abroad.

When she had a little boy, Aydan, she found that he too loved stories and wanted his mum, Farah, to tell him stories all the time. They had a favourite place for stories that was just behind Brick Lane, in a place called Allen Gardens. In this lovely green park, under a big magnolia tree, they would sit and story after story would be told.

One fine spring day Aydan said, 'Please Mum, can you tell me a story from Bangladesh?' And as Farah looked up at the beautiful flowers that were now in bloom on the magnolia tree, and as she breathed in their lovely perfume, she was reminded of the Champak tree that grows in Bangladesh. The Champak is very similar in looks and in smell to the magnolia tree and suddenly an old story that her grandmother used to tell her came to mind:

A long, long time ago in a place called Sunderpur there lived a king who had three wives. Well, that wasn't so unusual for a king in those days. But what was a bit unusual was that all his people loved him because he was always kind, helpful and gentle. Other kings weren't always so nice. Now, although *he* was liked by everybody, his first two wives were not. They were mean and selfish, and they were jealous of the third queen who was gentle and kind – and she was also the king's favourite.

Well, it seemed that the king had all that he could wish for. A people who loved him, three wives and a beautiful kingdom with mountains, green meadows and forests. But the one thing that he and his wives did not have was a child. This made them all sad, but the king was more than sad. Because he was a king, he thought he should have a little princess or a prince who could take over the kingdom after him.

And so, being depressed by this, he spent more and more of his time wandering on his own in the mountains and in the meadows and the forests of his land. One day he met a priest sitting underneath a mango tree. The priest told him that if he really wanted a child then he could give his wives the mangoes of childbearing, pointing to the tree above him. He gave the king three of its fruits and told him that his wives should each eat a mango and then they would each have a child.

When he got home he gave his three wives the fruits as instructed by the priest. The younger wife ate her fruit, believing that maybe it really would work and she would have a child, but the other two wives had a bite and spat out the rest. 'How stupid to believe that a mango will make you have a baby!' they said. However, the younger wife soon discovered that she *was* going to have a baby.

The king was overjoyed! He decided to treat everybody in his kingdom to celebrate this wonderful news. He gave presents to everyone in the palace and he made sure that all needy and poor people were given baskets of food and new clothes to wear. The whole kingdom was celebrating the good news. It was just as if, in every home, a child was going to be born into their own family.

But all this happiness that everyone else was feeling wasn't being shared by those two selfish people in the palace. These other two wives were now so jealous of the younger queen that they could no longer bear to look at her face. The king, however, became very fond of his favourite queen and to show his love for her, he gave her a golden bell. The bell was hanging from a golden chain and he said, 'My dear queen, after our child is born, whenever you need me, ring this bell and I shall be there beside you.' With these soft words, he left her in her room and returned to his work in the palace.

In the meantime, the other two wicked queens decided to be there when the youngest queen gave birth – and that is exactly what they did. But instead of just one baby, they were amazed to see that the queen had given birth to seven beautiful baby boys and a really lovely little girl. They took the newborn babies and quickly buried them in the forest outside the palace! However, the youngest queen knew nothing of this because she was so tired after having eight little babies that she fell into a deep sleep and had no chance of ringing the golden bell to let the king know the happy news.

Having done this terrible thing, the two wicked queens placed seven puppies and a crab beside the youngest queen. When she woke up, the youngest queen looked around her, expecting to see her babies. But there were only puppies and a crab.

The other queens laughed hoarsely. 'The king has always liked you more than us, but he'll soon change his mind when he sees you've had puppies and a crab instead of babies!' The shock was too much for the youngest queen to bear and she fainted. Then the first wicked queen rang the bell for the king to come. He rushed to be beside his young queen but he was horrified when, instead of a little baby, there were seven puppies and a crab beside her.

When the other two queens told him that his youngest wife had given birth to animals instead of babies, his excitement turned into rage. He immediately thought his youngest queen was a witch and he sent her away from his kingdom. The poor queen left the palace believing that she really had had animals instead of little babies. She was so unhappy, thinking that maybe there was something wrong with her.

The two older queens were delighted that their wicked plan had worked. The king by now became so confused and upset that he could no longer do the work of a king. When his ministers came to ask what they should do about problems in the country, he just wasn't able to tell them. He stopped caring for his people and he wandered lonely and sad in the woods and forests outside the palace.

Because of these terrible things that had happened to the queen and her babies, nature too became sad. The rivers dried up and the trees, flowers and vegetables shriveled up and stopped growing. People had nothing to eat and became sick with hunger and the king didn't know what to do. One day the king was walking unhappily through the dry and dying forest that once had been so green, when, in the middle of an area of scrubby twigs and brambles, he saw something that surprised him.

It was a single tree which had seven yellow flowers. They had the most lovely smell and above them, on the same tree, was a beautiful purple trumpet-shaped flower. He recognised these as seven Champak flowers and one Parul blossom. He remembered that these flowers used to grow so beautifully in his garden. All of a sudden, he felt close to these fresh and bright little flowers, as if they were his own children! But what he didn't know was that they really *were* his children!

You see, the seven Champak flowers were his seven sons and the Parul was his little daughter that the wicked queens had buried in the forest. After being in the ground, they had grown into these lovely flowers. He reached out to pick one of the Champak flowers. But as he did so the flowers scampered up the tree and the Parul sang out:

Rise up, rise up, oh brothers mine,
Rise up you princes, oh so fine,
Rise up high into the tree
And look who's here to pick you!

The seven Champak flowers asked, 'Sister Parul, should we let the king pick us?'

'No way!' said the Parul. 'Only our mother queen can touch us,' and the seven Champak flowers scampered to the top of the tree where Parul was.

'This is all very strange,' thought the king.

'Talking flowers! … and asking for a mother queen?' He sent for the first queen. Seeing her, the Parul flower sang her song and the brothers again asked if they should let the queen pick them. But again Parul answered, 'Only our mother queen can touch us.' The king sent for the second queen and the same thing happened: they would not let her pick them.

Now Parul called out, 'Oh King, bring our mother queen here and we will gladly fall into her arms.' Now the king was confused. Where was the youngest queen? Since he'd sent her away no one knew where she was. A search party was sent out and she was eventually found working as a servant in a neighbouring kingdom.

When she was brought to the tree and looked up at the beautiful flowers, they dropped into her hands, one by one. All at once, Parul turned into a beautiful princess and the seven Champak flowers into seven lovely princes. They all hugged this woman, saying, 'Oh Mother, we're finally all together.' The king looked at the woman standing there in ragged clothes surrounded by her eight delighted children and finally realised that she was the youngest queen that he had sent away.

When the boys told him of the cruelty
of the two wicked queens, he had them
banished from his kingdom, never to see
them again. He begged the youngest queen
for forgiveness and she, just as you might
expect from the kind and gentle person that
she was, forgave him. It took a long time for

Parul and her seven brothers to forgive their father, but when they saw how truly sorry he was, they and their mother and father lived happily ever after.

MAGIC WATER

Pernilla is a Londoner. But she wasn't born in London. She grew up in Sweden – but she wasn't born *there* either. You see, when she was a baby, she'd been found, wrapped in a blanket, on the streets of Seoul, the capital of Korea. She had been left there so that somebody would find her and take care of her. Well, there was a family in Sweden who wanted a baby so much that when they heard about her, they decided they would take her and bring her up as their own. So that tiny little girl travelled thousands of miles across the world to her new home in Sweden. They loved her, they cared for her and they helped her to grow.

And when she was old enough, she went to school. There she learnt with all the other children who, like many Swedish people, had blue eyes and blond hair. Pernilla had black hair and oriental eyes. But no one called her names or bullied her. Why should they? They just treated her like any other child in her school. She was Swedish just like them. Anyway, when she came home

from school, she would always draw and colour, even before she did her homework. She just loved art and wanted to be an artist when she grew up.

When she was twelve, the family had a holiday in London. Pernilla liked London and she liked Tina who showed them around. Tina was a young Swedish woman who lived and worked in London. This was such a great idea to Pernilla and she decided that she would like to come and live in this great city and become an artist – and that's exactly what happened. She came to

London to live and to work here and she became an artist, just like she had always wanted. Pernilla shows her paintings in galleries and exhibitions in London and all around the world, and she just loves being a Londoner.

And because all of these things happened to her when she was little, she always feels very close to this story which comes from Korea. That's because there is something in the story that makes her think of her own life. It's one of her all-time favourites:

An old man and woman lived in a poor house at the edge of a forest. They were very loving to each other and to all their neighbours around them. Their only sadness was that they had no children who could help them grow their vegetables, chop the wood, or mend things in the house. And so all the love that they had, they would share with the people around them. Their nearest neighbour was a rich man who lived in a large house. He had fine clothes and had as much good food to eat as he liked – but he was also mean and greedy.

Even so, they would always be nice to him and share with him the little that they had. Whatever they grew in their garden, they would always take the first of what they had grown to him. They'd knock on his door and say, 'Dear neighbour, these are our first spring lettuces and, because you are our neighbour, they are for you.' He would grunt and take them. Then he'd close the door and wouldn't even say thank you.

In the autumn, when they roasted the chestnuts from their old tree, they'd take the first tasty chestnuts to him before they'd even eaten any themselves. He would open the door saying, 'Oh, it's you. What do you want?'

The same would happen again: he would shut the door in their faces and he wouldn't say thank you. But even though he never thanked them, they would still be kind to him. They were really kind and loving people.

One very cold winter when the snow was falling hard, they were trying to keep warm in front of the little fire in their tiny house. Their hands were warm but the rest of them was so very, very cold. The old woman looked in the corner where they piled the

firewood and she saw that there were only a few sticks left. 'If we don't get any more wood tonight, we'll surely freeze to death.'

The old man agreed, saying he'd go and get some. 'But do be careful,' said the old woman, 'you don't walk so well any more, and it's so icy you could slip and break your leg.'

But what could he do? They had to get some wood and they needed it soon, so he stepped out slowly on his tired old legs into the forest. There was so much snow that all the sticks were buried under the snow. The few sticks that he did find were wet and would be too hard to burn. Then suddenly he heard the whistling of a bird. It was chirping and singing and when he looked up he saw it was flitting from branch to branch. He thought it strange to see a beautiful songbird in the middle of winter, but as it flew deeper into the forest he followed it.

The bird came to a stop and sang and sang as if it was saying, 'Look down!' When the old man did look down he saw that there was a fountain of water coming out of the ice. By now he was tired and very thirsty, so he took a little scoop of water in his hand and noticed that it was clear and sweet and not even cold. After he had drunk, he suddenly felt very tired and before he knew it, he was sleeping against a tree, lying on the ice.

When he woke up he remembered that he should be collecting firewood. He jumped up with so much energy and started clearing snow, finding wood underneath it. His legs felt strong and he went straight back home feeling very energetic.

When he got home his wife said, 'Oh, my goodness, what's happened? You've become a young man again! Just feel your face, it's so soft and smooth.' When he felt his face, he noticed there was not a single wrinkle.

'It's true! It must've been the water. Come with me and you can become young too!' And that's just what happened. She went with him, drank the water and became a young woman again.

Next morning when the rich neighbour looked over his garden fence he saw lots of activity in his neighbours' garden. They were very busy shovelling the snow, sweeping the yard and mending the roof of the little house. He went straight over and said, 'Who are you? Where are my old neighbours?' Being the kind and loving people they were, they told him everything that had happened to them.

Before they'd even finished speaking, their neighbour was running towards the forest, wanting to drink some of this magic water himself. Well that was in the morning, but now it was almost four o'clock and the old woman said to her husband, 'He's been away all day. He must've got lost, or maybe he's fallen on the ice and broken his leg. It's starting to get dark now, we should go and see if we can find him.' But when they got to the place where the water was, they couldn't see him. All they saw was a pile of clothes, *his* clothes.

'Oh dear, some wild animal has killed him, and all that is left is his clothes!' said the woman. But then they heard the crying sound of a baby coming from the clothes. The neighbour who'd always been mean and greedy had drunk so much water that instead of just becoming younger, he'd become a little baby! The woman looked at her husband and said, 'Maybe this is the child we have always wanted. We should take him home and look after him.'

They picked up the baby, cuddled him and took him home and cared for him. They brought him up as their own child: he was

their own and they were his parents. When that baby grew up, everyone said what a kind and generous person he was. Maybe now he had the love that he didn't have before and, having that love, he was now able to give love back in return.

The Tower of London has been a royal residence, an armoury, a mint (a place where coins are made), a menagerie, an observatory and a safe deposit box for the crown jewels.

The Raven's eye saw the Tower rise,
In the risen Tower, the raven's cry.
In the raven's cry, the gusting wind,
In the gusting wind, the raven's eye.
Over the spacious earth they fly
To tell the stories of times gone by.

Hello, we are ravens, we are sisters. My name is Munin, which means 'memory', and my sister's name is Hugin, which means 'thought'. We live in the Tower of London, next to the River Thames. We have a lot to think about and a lot to remember.

When the mist rises from the river, the battlements, the walls, the White Tower appears and disappears in the drifting mist. Figures from the past seem to walk through solid stone. When the tide rides high, the smells of salt and seaweed are borne on the wind.

We are well named: thought and memory. We ravens are clever birds and living here gives us a lot to think about, a lot of stories

to tell. Some of the stories you will have heard, of how in 1536 we ravens sat silent and immovable on the battlements and gazed eerily at the strange scene of a queen about to die. We will tell you no more of this or of the cruelties powerful kings and queens have visited upon others.

You know humans refer to a lot of ravens together as 'an unkindness of ravens'. Ironic, as we ravens have never – and could never – be as unkind as some humans are. We are faithful to each other and if one of us dies, we mourn and grieve. We can mimic human speech. We have conversations with each other and take it in turn to listen. We love to play. Sometimes we like to trick the visitors. One time a raven called Bran lay on his back, perfectly still, with his claws in the air, his eyes shut. The visitors thought he was dead and ran to get help, but he was only fooling. I think we could be called:

'A playfulness of ravens'
or
'A cleverness of ravens'
or
'A faithfulness of ravens'

What do you think?

But back to the stories of the past. Doesn't everything die at last and too soon? But here every night, when the ghostly shadows emerge cautiously from Tower Green, the Roman city wall and the White Tower, they share with us the stories of their wild and precious lives.

In the year 1101 there was a bishop, an important priest of the Church, imprisoned in the Tower. His name was Ranulf Flambard. He had with him some of the church wine. It was strong wine and it wasn't difficult for him to persuade the guards to drink it. They had one drink, two drinks, three drinks then they fell to the floor. Then Ranulf Flambard (what a wonderful name!) tied a rope to the edge of the cell window and escaped by climbing down the rope.

About 600 years later, the Earl of Nithsdale was in the Tower. He and other Scottish lords had rebelled against the king. He was there awaiting execution when his wife and two of her friends were allowed to visit him. Well, they were clever women and they were determined to free the earl. The women went backwards and forwards to their carriage to fetch things for the earl and perhaps they also gave the guards some nice things to eat. Sometimes they had veils covering their faces, sometimes they wore different coloured cloaks.

The guards were unsure how many of them there were and anyway, they didn't think they had to be too worried as they were very polite and gentle ladies. Well, those ladies had brought women's clothes for the earl to put on. They had a fine lady's hat for him to wear and they covered the stubble on his chin with a lot of make-up. They left the Tower with the guards opening and holding the door for them. It was only when later the guards checked the cell they saw that the Earl of Nithsdale had escaped.

We ravens love that story. Must have been like a pantomime.

Some years before that, a man with the splendid name of Colonel Thomas Blood broke into the Tower and made off with a golden orb, a sceptre and a crown. He was caught, but King Charles the Second pardoned him. Colonel Blood was allowed to go free. Maybe there had been enough blood spilt in King Charles's own family history and he would rather concentrate on having a good time. In fact, he was famous for having a good time.

But when we ravens think of the past, a lot of what we share with each other are the stories of the animals who have lived at the Tower.

It was 1252 and very dark and bitter cold upon the Thames; the east wind blowing bleak and bringing with it the scent of marsh and moor and fen. We felt his presence before we saw him. It was a great white bear. One leg was chained and a collar and chain around his neck. He was all alone, no partner, no other of his kind. He came from a land of ice and snow, given as a gift to the king. They led him down to the Thames every day so that he could swim and catch fish, but he was never free. A rope was attached to his collar when he swam.

Poor beast. He did not live long and neither did the elephant that was brought here a few years later. All the way from Africa on a swaying sailing ship, unloaded at the docks to come and stay here at the Tower. Huge, intelligent beast. Brought here as a gift for the king. He would swing his great head from side to side and lift one foot up at a time.

He was chained, of course. He died after a couple of years. When we remember these things, the sky grows dark and thunderous.

But you know, what humans do and don't do matters very little to the river and the land. The river flows on, the tide rises and falls. In the early morning the geese follow the old paths. In centuries gone by, they flew above marsh and fen, then market gardens and villages, now streets and houses and tall glass office blocks.

As for we two sisters, we have lived here a while along with the other five ravens. The Ravenmaster feeds us well. We have raw meat twice a day, biscuits soaked in blood and fresh fruit. We live well and we have long lives, but Hugin, my sister, has died. We ravens mourned. I stood by her for three days and touched my beak to Hugin's closed eyes. Then I needed to be on my own for a while. I escaped and flew to Greenwich. Greenwich is not that far from the Tower if you fly following the river. I was brought back after five days.

I am here still and we ravens continue to guard the Tower and tell the stories of times gone by in this great city of London.

Society *for*
Storytelling

Since 1993, The Society for Storytelling has championed the ancient art of oral storytelling and its long and honourable history – not just as entertainment, but also in education, health, and inspiring and changing lives. Storytellers, enthusiasts and academics support and are supported by this registered charity to ensure the art is nurtured and developed throughout the UK.

Many activities of the Society are available to all, such as locating storytellers on the Society website, taking part in our annual National Storytelling Week at the start of every February, purchasing our quarterly magazine Storylines, or attending our Annual Gathering – a chance to revel in engaging performances, inspiring workshops, and the company of like-minded people.

You can also become a member of the Society to support the work we do. In return, you receive free access to Storylines, discounted tickets to the Annual Gathering and other storytelling events, the opportunity to join our mentorship scheme for new storytellers, and more. Among our great deals for members is a 30% discount off titles from The History Press.

For more information, including how to join, please visit

www.sfs.org.uk